I'm Reading About The IDITAROD

GALLOPADE

by Carole Marsh

Printed and Manufactured in Peachtree City, GA., USA www.gallopade.com

Book design: Susan Van Denhende

Editor: Janice Baker

Photo Credits: Cover: Bill King/Bigstock.com. Page 3: iclipart.com. Pages 5A, 18B, 20, 24B, 26B, 32A, 34: Frank Kovalchek CC BY 2.0. Page 5B: U.S. Air Force. Pages 9 & 11A: Library of Congress. Page 11B: jim.henderson/Wikimedia Commons. Page 13: kborozinski/Bigstock.com. Page 15: Gray_alaska.png/Wikimedia Commons. Page 17: Kamchatka-Peninsula/Bigstock.com. Pages 18A & 32B: flickr user ra64 CC BY-SA 2.0. Page 22: David Weekly CC BY 2.0. Page 24A: ZdenekK CC BY-SA 3.0. Pages 24C & 32C: James Brooks CC BY 2.0. Page 26A: Alexey Ushatsky/Bigstock.com; 26C: Josef Pittner/Bigstock.com. Page 27: iclipart.com. Page 28: Bering Land Bridge National Preserve CC BY 2.0. Page 30: Reiter, Jennifer. *Congratulations to Noah!* blog post, 2013 at https://dancingdownthetrail.wordpress.com; accessed October 2016.

The Iditarod Trail Sled Dog Race is an amazing event!

What is so special about the Iditarod?

Let's read about it and see!

INTRODUCTION

The Iditarod Trail Sled Dog Race
is a famous sled dog race!
Its nickname is "the Iditarod."

Every year, teams of sled dogs and their mushers
dash across the state of Alaska.
They brave the frigid weather
and rugged wilderness for up to two weeks!

The drivers guiding the dog teams
are known as "mushers."

The Iditarod

LOCATION

Alaska is the largest state in the United States! Much of Alaska is wilderness where few people live. It is home to snow-capped mountains, vast glaciers, lush forests, and thousands of rushing rivers.

In 1867, Russia sold Alaska to the United States. Alaska became the 49th state in 1959—almost 100 years later!

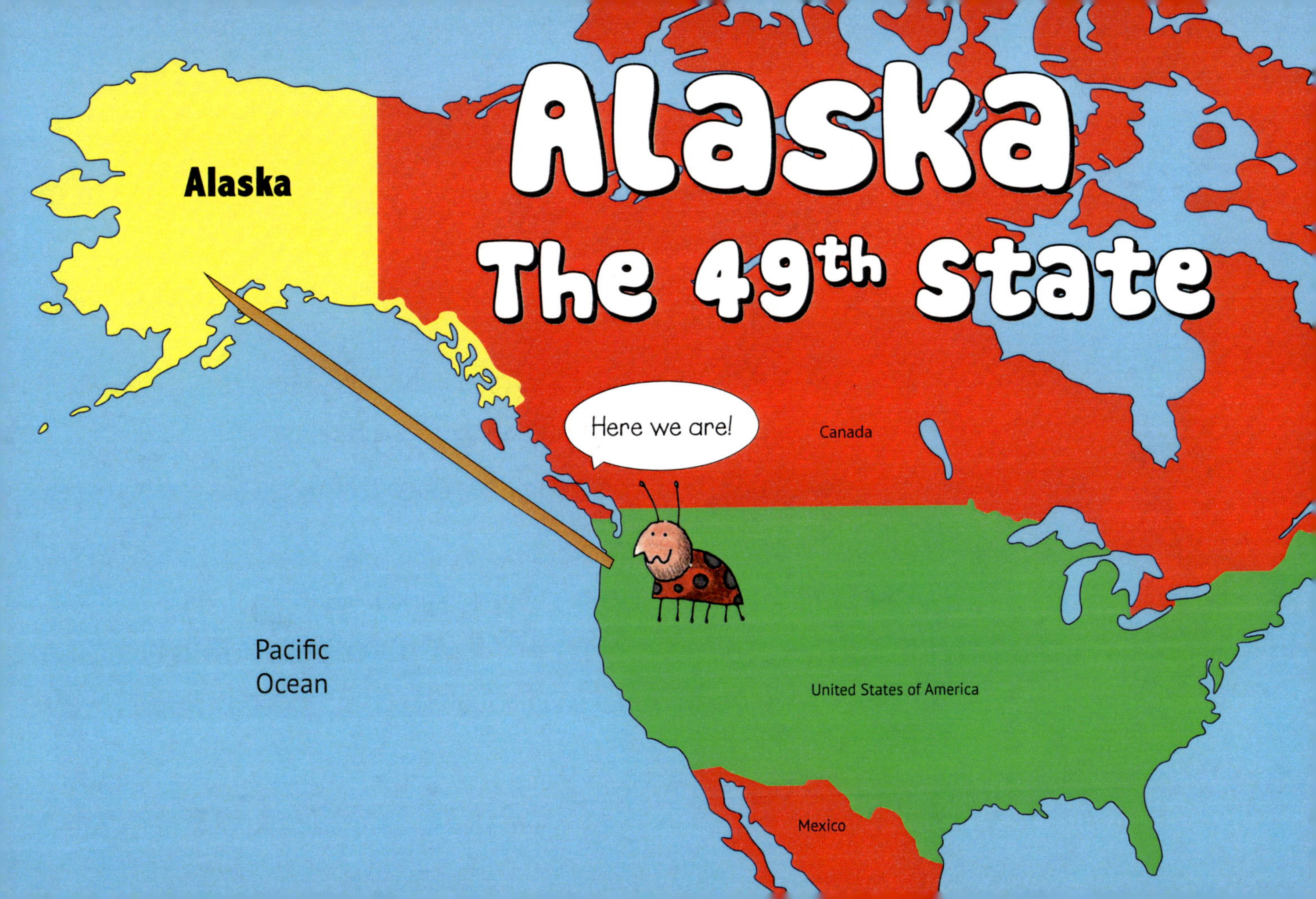
Alaska
The 49th State
Alaska
Here we are!
Canada
Pacific Ocean
United States of America
Mexico

HISTORY

Long ago, Alaska had few roads.
People needed sled dogs to survive!

The Iditarod Trail began as a route
for mail and supplies.
The trail connected small settlements,
trading posts, and mining camps.

Sled dog teams carried mail and supplies
from towns on the coast to the middle of Alaska.
Those dogs served as a lifeline for Alaskans!

Carrying the Mail

HISTORY

In 1925, sled dog teams used part of the Iditarod Trail to save the lives of children in Alaska.

A deadly disease called diphtheria broke out in Nome, Alaska. Doctors needed a special serum to cure the disease, but the closest supplies were 700 miles away.

Teams of sled dogs and mushers worked in a relay. They got the medicine to Nome in six days!

The famous sled dog Balto led his team on the final leg of the relay!

Sled Dogs Deliver

Statue of Balto

IDITAROD BEGINS

The Iditarod Trail Sled Dog Race began in 1973. A musher named Joe Redington, Sr. worked hard to launch the annual race. He is known as the "Father of the Iditarod."

The Iditarod was started for several reasons:

- To preserve the historic Iditarod Trail from Seward to Nome
- To save the sled dog culture in Alaska and Alaskan huskies, which were being phased out in Alaska thanks to snowmobiles

The Race Begins

MAP

The Iditarod begins near Anchorage.
It starts on the first weekend in March.
Mushers and dogs travel around 1,000 miles
to the finish line in Nome.

The Iditarod course crosses massive mountains,
thick forests, and even frozen rivers!

There are two routes: northern and southern.
Racers take the northern route in even years.
Racers take the southern route in odd years.

Iditarod Routes

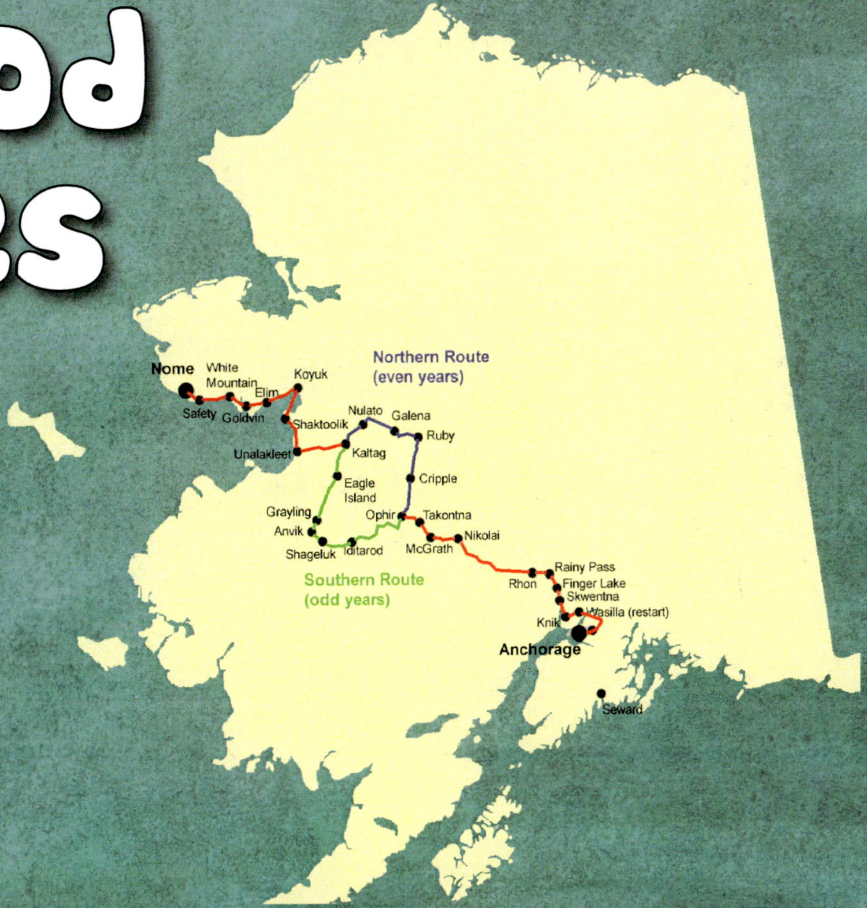

TEAMWORK

Iditarod dog teams usually have 12 to 16 dogs.

The dogs run in pairs on either side of a "gangline." That line is attached to their harnesses and the sled.

Mushers put the dogs in the best place for their abilities. For example, the lead dogs must be alert and intelligent. The wheel dogs must be strong and easygoing. They are carrying hundred of pounds behind them!

Experienced mushers frequently have dogs change their positions during the race!

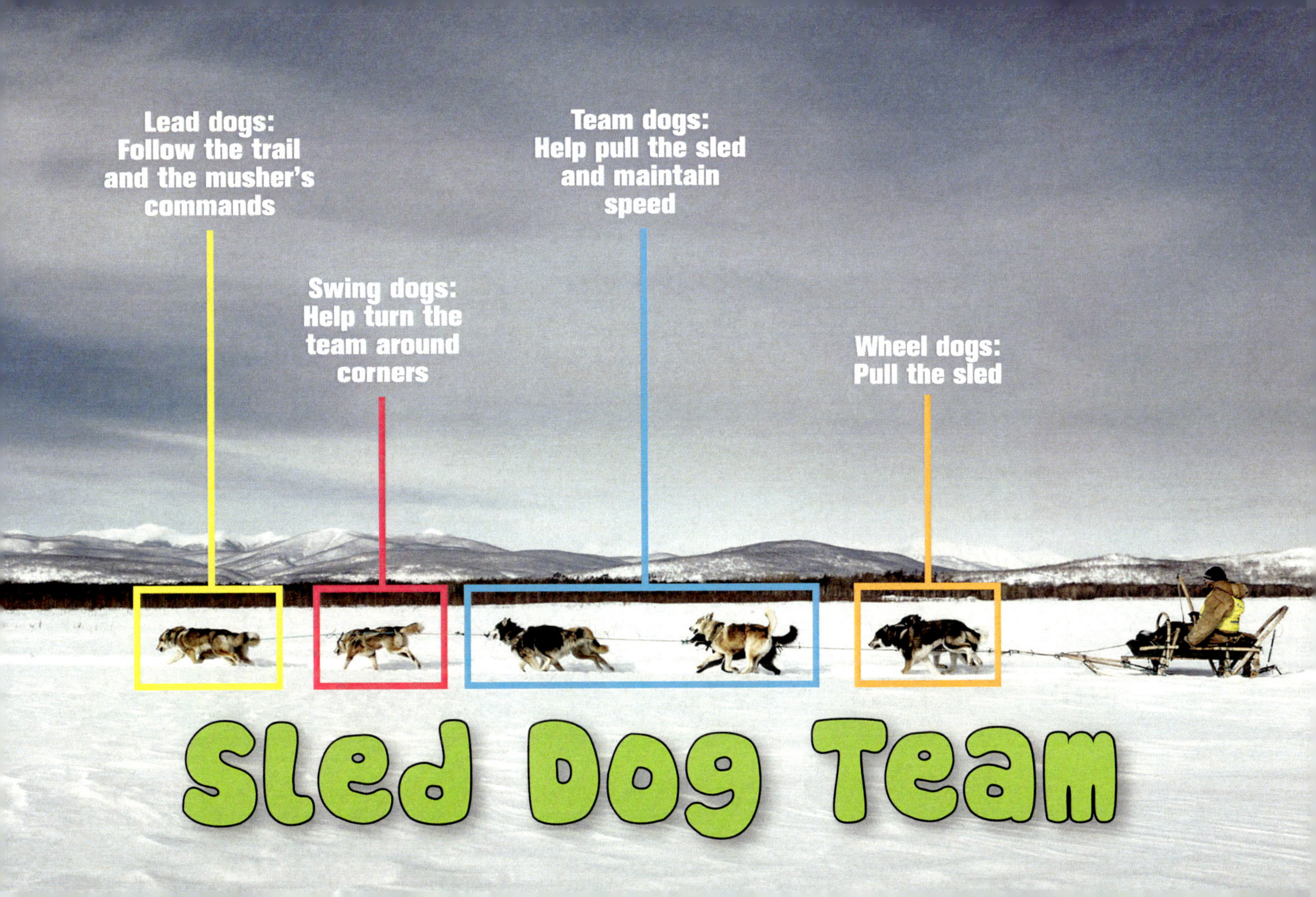
Lead dogs: Follow the trail and the musher's commands
Swing dogs: Help turn the team around corners
Team dogs: Help pull the sled and maintain speed
Wheel dogs: Pull the sled
Sled Dog Team

Dogs with Booties

Mushing Across Alaska

SLEDS AND SUPPLIES

Mushers stand on the back of their sleds and call orders to their dog teams.

Sleds may be made of wood or newer, space-age materials. Mushers pack them with supplies like:

Cooking Pot **Ax** **Sleeping Bag** **Snowshoes** **Dog Booties**

Mush!

COMMANDS

Mushers have special commands for their dogs:

Gee! = Turn Right
Haw! = Turn Left
Easy! = Slow Down
Whoa! = Stop
Mush! Hike! Let's Go! All Right! = Go
On By! = Pass another team or other distraction

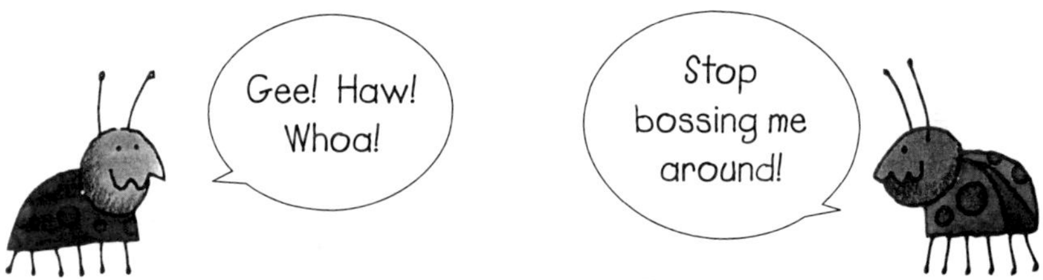

Time to Rest

During the race, mushers stop at checkpoints.
There, the dogs eat, and sleep on beds of straw.

What does a sled dog eat? A LOT!
Before the race, mushers ship food to the checkpoints.
Each musher has a special formula
including dry dog food, meat, fats, and vitamins.
Mushers add liquid and cook the food into a tasty gruel.

Alaskan Husky

HUSKY

The most common type of dog in the Iditarod
is the "Alaskan husky."
Alaskan huskies are known for speed and endurance!

Many mushers own their own kennels
and raise their own dogs.
The best sled dogs have a good attitude.
They are happy, smart, and eager to run!

Dangerous Trail

Braving the Weather

Watch for Moose!

DANGERS

There are many dangers along the Iditarod Trail!
Some dangers include:

- Below-zero temperatures, snowstorms, and biting wind
- Falling through the ice over a frozen lake or river
- Attacks by animals like moose and wolves
- Treacherous, slippery trails with rocks and trees

FINISH
Alaska Airlines
KONICA MINOLTA
ANCHORAGE
ExxonMobil
HORIZON LINES
ANCHORAGE
END OF IDITAROD SLED DOG RACE
NOME
1049
MILES

The Winner!

The winner of the Iditarod crosses under
an arch made from a spruce log.
It is known as the "Burled Arch."
What a great sight it must be!

The "Widow's Lamp" hangs from the arch.
Race officials light it when the race starts.
They put it out when the last musher finishes.

The last-place finisher gets the
Red Lantern Award for perseverance!

Junior Iditarod

JR. IDITAROD

The Junior Iditarod is a race for teens!
Mushers from 14 to 17 years old can be in the race.
The route is 140 miles long.
It covers the first 70 miles of the main Iditarod Trail.

Mushers and their dogs stay overnight
and head back the next day.
It is a great way for young mushers to learn
what it takes to be in the famous Iditarod race!

Scenes from the Trail

Movin' Along

Wear your Booties!

Dog Tired

DID YOU KNOW?

Read these fascinating facts about the Iditarod:

- The Iditarod is a National Historic Trail.
- The race usually lasts between 9 and 15 days.
- Sled dogs travel about 5–12 miles per hour.
- If a dog is tired or injured, it rides in the sled.
- The winner gets a cash prize and a new truck!

Amazing Race!

AMAZING RACE

The Iditarod Trail Sled Dog Race is called
"The Last Great Race on Earth."

The Iditarod is an amazing race
across awesome Alaska!
It takes special people and special dogs
to run such a race:

Brave **Strong** **Fearless** **Determined** **Prepared**

GLOSSARY

endurance: the ability to go on under pain or hardship

frigid: extremely cold

gangline: a central line that connects a sled to the individual tuglines of the animals pulling the sled

glacier: a slowly moving mass of ice

gruel: a thin liquid food

lifeline: a thing on which someone or something depends

perseverance: continued effort to do something despite difficulties; not giving up

relay: an act of passing something along from one person, group, or station to another